Mary's Real L

I've changed her name to protect the litt
but people who drink in The Clock or liv
know who I'm talking about. Mary wasn't always an oul
argumentative drunk. There's always a backstory, which is rarely told.

Like many of us, Mary danced in the National, the Ierne, enjoyed the cabaret in the Tudor Rooms or the Wexford Inn. She met her future husband, Paddy, in the Ierne on a Saturday night, and she was madly in love. The problem was that Paddy was from Co. Laois, just up in Dublin for the weekend. Somehow, when they got married he persuaded Mary to give up her familiar life in Dublin and move to the country.

Well, she was a fish out of water. She couldn't understand the accent of these culchies. She was lonely, but stuck it out because she loved Paddy so much. When she became pregnant, it seemed like a dream come true. The birth of her son, John, only added to her isolation though. She wanted her Mam around to offer advice and just confirm she was being a good mother.

Shortly after John's first birthday Mary made the decision to move back to Dublin. Paddy was having none of it. He wanted his son to inherit the small farm. Well, it all ended up in the courts, and Mary lost. Young John was to stay on the farm with his father.

Mary had a choice to make. She could stay with Paddy and John, or move back to her hometown, Dublin. She thought that John was better provided for on the farm, so made the hard choice - to leave him behind. As John grew up, his Dad discouraged him from contacting Mary and eventually the letters stopped.

We just never know what other people have suffered in their lives. Be kind to someone today.

People have been asking if Mary ever saw her son John again. The short answer is yes she did, but it didn't go well. Paddy died about 12 years ago, and John came up to Dublin to see her. He was around 23 at that stage, and they hadn't met for a few years. She was so nervous, she started drinking a bit too early in the day, with the result she was quite pissed when John arrived. He wasn't impressed. He asked her if she'd move back to Laois with him. He clearly wanted to build bridges. Mary, though, said no. A decision, I think, she regrets every day.

John wrote a few times, but she never replied, and I guess he just gave up. He's married now with a couple of kids that Mary's never seen.

I called round to her today, and she's in a bad way, but there's only so much you can do. All her friends just feel helpless. There isn't a happy ending to every story. Mary doesn't know this, but I've kept in touch with John. A letter around Christmas. He tried his best to stay in touch with her, but it seemed she's closed down that part of her life. He is happily married and has a couple of kids. Mary has never seen them.

Her and I met in the Ierne back in the day. She fancied my friend Ronnie from Ballyfermot, so obviously she asked me to dance. We knew straight away we weren't boyfriend/girlfriend, but she had a wicked sense of humour. She got off with Ronnie that night, but nothing more was said, so I suppose it wasn't a happy ending.

She was a regular in the Tudor Rooms as well. Her and her friend Bernie would often join me and my Beaumont squeeze M, Jaysus 3 women at the same table! They were good times indeed. Then of course, Mary met Paddy and moved down to the wilds of Laois.

I think Mary knew quite quickly she'd made a big mistake moving to Laois. At that stage, there was a gang of us who'd meet up in the Tudor Rooms, from all over Dublin. Some of the group had already paired off, the rest of us still single and carefree. Mary was used to calling in to her Mam a few times a week for a cup of tea and a chat.

That was all gone. The house was a couple of miles outside the town, with no neighbours close by. Paddy, of course, was working during the day, and sometimes into the evening too. She'd grown up in a block of flats, so knew nothing about gardening. The vegetable plot soon became overgrown. I think it was then that she started drinking during the day, just to relieve the loneliness.

Then young John arrived. I'm not a mother, obviously, but I know from family that even in the city it can be an isolating experience. Mary just wanted her Mammy around to teach her about being a Mam herself, and just to care. She had to raise John by instinct. It turned out that Paddy was very traditional when it came to children - it was Mary's job, and she just had to get on with it.

I don't know how long it to took before Mary began to think of coming home. She came up one weekend and joined us at the Tudor Rooms. It was great to see her relax and enjoy herself. She got an idea of what she'd been missing. The decision was made. Of course, Paddy wasn't giving up his only son. She knew she'd struggle to provide for John, and was heartbroken to leave him behind. A selfish choice? Walk a mile in her shoes.

Mary moved in with her Mam in Pimlico for a little while before she got a small (and I mean **small**) bedsit off Francis St. She got a job in a shoe shop on Meath St, and I suppose that's when she started drinking in the Clock. Her and I had clicked from that first night in the Tudor Rooms, and always tried to stay in touch.

She was missing young John terribly. By this time, she had no communication with Paddy, which broke her heart. She still loved him, but just couldn't hack daily life down in Laois. We'd meet up in the Clock a couple of times a week. She was always good fun. She was the first person I told I was gay. She wasn't at all surprised. "You were just too fuckin' nice to be straight", was her reply. She was also the first to meet my partner, John. What is with 'husband' nowadays? I never wanted a husband. If I wanted a husband, I'd become a woman and do it right.

I went around to see Mary last night. She was feeling very fragile - emotionally, I mean. She was mortified about being barred from the Clock, she felt she couldn't show her face around the area. Now, I think the last thing she needed to was hide away. I'd had a word with Tom, the owner, and he said she'd be welcome back, if she wanted. He made it clear, though, that she'd be 'on probation' - any more trouble and she'd be barred for good.

It took a lot of coaxing, but she eventually agreed to go around for a couple of pints. It was quiet enough, luckily. I ordered the drinks and we sat in the corner. A couple of her friends came over to say hello, which was great. She began to relax a bit. This wasn't the time to confront her about what had happened, or whether she'd go back to rehab. She just needed a friend, and because she'd been a good friend to me over the years, I was happy to help. I felt sure that, given time, we could get her through this rough patch. Let's hope so, anyway.

Chicken or egg? Did Mary's drinking fuck up her life? Or did her fucked up life lead to Mary's drinking? Does it matter any more? Not really. If you were around in those days, you know every group had its stars. Mary was one of ours. The other was Nadger Smith from down the hill on Cook Street. Jayz, he was gorgeous. He was also great fun - a born entertainer. Who wouldn't love him? There were lots of broken hearts (mine included) when he emigrated to Canada with his family.

Anyway, we're talking about Mary. When she moved back to Dublin she felt as isolated and alone as she'd felt in Laois. And she was missing her son so much. I was in the first flush of romance with my new man (now my old man!) so we only saw each other maybe once a week. Sometimes, we didn't see each other for a couple of weeks. Jeez, where does the responsibility lie for keeping friendships on track? I've no idea. I do know I've disappointed people, like Mary, because I was too busy enjoying my new gay life. I was also hurt by friends who didn't keep in touch.

When her day's work in the shop was over, Mary faced the decision - go back to her grotty little room and cook food she didn't want, or go to the pub and meet friends for chat and drinks. What choice would you make?

Jack and I were happily settling into our new life in Ranelagh. My visits to the Clock to see Mary became less frequent. I still feel guilty about that, but at the time I was just living my life. Mary met a man, Richard, in the Clock one night. He was a big bruiser of a man. I don't know what she saw in him. To be honest, I never liked him. Of course, he didn't like me either - fucking queers, I could hear him say in his tiny mind.

She seemed happy for a few months. Do you remember 'The Woman Who Walked Into Doors' by Roddy Doyle? That was Mary. The first time she arrived in the Clock with a black eye, she said she'd banged into a cupboard door. Then Richard learned the classic abusers rule - hit them where the bruises won't show. She could explain away the little gasps of pain in her ribs when she reached for her pint. I started to have my suspicions - I'd grown up with an alcoholic father. I guess I left it too late to confirm those suspicions.

She had to call an ambulance herself because your man had legged it. She was brought the short distance to James' Hospital. It turned out she had a ruptured spleen from where the bastard had kicked her. She gave me as her next of kin (her Mam had died by this time) so the hospital called me.

In the taxi over I kind of knew what had happened. She looked in a bad way. No obvious injury, but very weak. I hate that when you go to a hospital you can't cry. You 'have to be strong' for the patient. I cried when I saw her. "Ah Mary", I said, "what's he done to you?"

She couldn't speak. She was in a lot of pain, and they'd given her painkillers while they waited for her to go to surgery. It was going to be a long day.

I was sitting with Mary about a week after her surgery. It had gone well but she'd need time to heal, emotionally as well as physically. Who should walk in only the bastard Richard. He's a lot bigger than me, but I was so angry.

"Get the fuck out of here", I shouted. "If you come near her again, you'll end up in the 'Joy".

"I'm really sorry", says he, and walked away. I was fucking livid.

When she was discharged from hospital, Mary came to stay with Jack and I. She was healing physically, but emotionally she was in bits. She'd lost the love of her life, Paddy. She'd lost her only child, John. She'd just been put in hospital by a man she cared about. She was lost.

Jack and I were both working, so she was on her own all day. That's when the drinking got bad. When she was able, she'd go for a walk, but too often it ended up in the pub. She'd bring home a bottle of cheap wine. When we came home, she was drunk and crying. It was heartbreaking, and we just didn't know how to help. What can you do in that situation?

We had a good friend, Tom, a GP who lived with his partner Paul a few doors up the avenue. We'd meet for dinner a couple of times a month in a little restaurant in Ranelagh village. Mary had moved back to her little bedsit, and was basically just drinking all the time. She'd long ago lost her job in the shoe shop on Meath Street.

I asked Tom one night during dinner, "what can I do to help her?". I don't want to belittle what he said, it's the standard answer (and really the only answer) - "You just have to wait until she reaches rock bottom, and admits she has a problem" Do nothing is what I heard. I wasn't happy with that. We all want to do something when our friends are in pain. But Tom was right. Do nothing, except be a friend, be there when she called, drunk, at 3 in the morning. Jesus, it was tough.

After a few months, Mary was barely keeping it together when we met in the Clock. I was beginning to hear stories of her becoming quite aggressive with old friends. I felt I had to do something and started bringing up the idea of her going into rehab. I didn't mention that in the pub, I'm not fucking stupid. I knew she'd kick off, and she did. But I felt that, deep down, she wanted someone to tell her how to change her life. The first step of the AA Programme talks about your life becoming unmanageable. That certainly applied to Mary.

I had checked out a couple of places. Jesus, it's not cheap! I couldn't understand why the HSE will fund treatment for drug addiction, but not alcohol addiction. An Irish solution. There was no point talking to her when she was drunk, so I'd go around to her place first thing in the morning, when she was at her most vulnerable. I admit I put a lot of pressure on her, but I was doing what I thought was best for her.

Obviously, I'm not going to name the centre. We visited a couple of times, so she could meet the staff, and go through the assessment procedure. I was excluded from that part. I was happy, though, to hand it over to the professionals. The place itself seemed really comfortable - modern but homely, if that makes sense.

Finally, she agreed to go in. It meant 6 weeks of no communication with friends or family. No phone calls, no texts. That was hard for me - I can't imagine what it must have been like for her. All we could do, then, was wait and see, and hope.

The only comfort we could take was that she was in good hands, and being taken care of. Eventually, I was allowed to visit. She looked well, physically, maybe had even put on a couple of pounds. We got a coffee and went out to the garden to chat. We'd known each other for over 20 years but this just felt so awkward.

"Look Jim", she said. "I have to thank you for all you've done for me". "Don't be silly"

"No. You don't understand. It's part of the programme. Making amends".

"Mary, you'd have done the same for me if I needed help". "Of course I would", she said, "but you didn't. I did, and you were there for me".

"Okay. I accept your thanks, and I'll do it again if you need help, but please, don't go down that road again".

"All I can do is try".

She stayed another 2 weeks in the centre. We'd agreed with the counsellor that she'd come and stay with us, but for a maximum of another 2 weeks. She needed to start taking responsibility for herself. I'd already taken a lot of time off work, and really couldn't afford any more. My boss was really understanding, but in the commercial world, there are limits.

Mary was going to 2 AA meeting every day. The recommendation for new members is 90 meetings in the first 90 days. Obviously, she couldn't talk about what had been said, but she told us it was helping. I took her at her word. Apparently, it was recommended that new members find a 'sponsor' - a member who'd a couple of years sobriety behind them. Mary connected with a woman called Joan. We never met, but they seemed to get on well.

To be honest, I was kind of glad to hand her over to someone else's care. I knew I hadn't really been there for Jack over the past couple of months. Too often, he ended up eating alone, or on the nights out with Tom and Paul, it was just the 3 of them. I needed to make it up to him. I suggested a long weekend away in Nice. We booked cheap flights but treated ourselves to a nice hotel. I'd told Mary that my phone would be switched off while I was away - this was me and Jack time. Ah, it was wonderful - we were romantic, silly like a couple of teenagers, just so relaxed. It was just what we needed.

Of course we talked about Mary. He made it clear that he completely understood my position, and he totally respected me for sticking with her. It was a relief to hear. I was under no illusion that AA would be the end of the dramas.

She seemed to be doing well. She'd done her 90 meetings in 90 days. She was seeing Joan a couple of times a week. Now when we met, it was for coffee, not pints. Maybe this time she'd actually make it? Yeah right, who were we kidding? After 6 months, she didn't so much fall off the wagon, but jump head first.

We've come full circle in this sorry tale. I got a call from the police. She was in Kilmainham Garda Station, having lost the head big time in the Clock. She'd spilled a load of drink, upended tables, the works. The Garda asked me if I'd take responsibility for her, so they could release her. I looked across at Jack and said no. It was probably the hardest thing I've ever done, but I knew Jack had a limit - after all, she was my friend, not his - and he was more important to me. I told the Garda that she'd just have to face the consequences of what she'd done.

The consequences were a trip to the District Court the next morning. She was fined €100, and ordered to pay €250 in damages to the Clock for the damage. I had thought about taking another day off work to be with her, but decided to let her face it alone. Shock tactics, I suppose. There's a term used about addiction called an enabler - someone who constantly helps the addict to avoid the real results of their actions. I had to face the fact I'd become Mary's enabler.

All that turned out to be beside the point. About 10 days after her court appearance, I got another phone call. This time it was from James' Hospital. Mary had been hit by a car on Patrick Street, and had been pronounced DOA - Dead On Arrival. It was evening time, and Jack was preparing dinner - he was the cook, I was the bottle washer. We immediately drove up to the hospital to see her.

Luckily (?) her head hadn't be injured, it was mainly her lower body. You know, she finally looked at peace. Sounds strange, doesn't it? Obviously, the first person I called was her son John. He said he'd be up first thing in the morning, and we agreed to meet at a nearby coffee shop before going to the hospital. He hadn't seen her in a few years, but he agreed she looked peaceful. He asked if I would organise the funeral. I was only too happy to do it. That sounds wrong, but you know what I mean.

None of us were religious, so we didn't have a Mass, we just went straight from the funeral home to Mount Jerome for the cremation.

There were a few old timers from the Clock, but it was sparsely attended. Back in the day, Mary had been a big Liverpool fan, so You'll Never Walk Alone was played. The 'ceremony' didn't last long. We went across the street to the pub and had a few drinks. Don't worry, John's wife wasn't drinking, so she drove them home about 2 o'clock, in time for the kids coming in from school.

John and Clare kept in touch, and Jack and I became the 'gay uncles' to their kids. He doesn't talk about Mary much, but I could never forget her.

Jack Wants A Baby!

I suppose like many gay men I've thought about what kind of father I would have made. I concluded I wouldn't be a good one - too selfish, too fond of my holidays. When I lived in England I donated sperm to a lesbian friend, and she had a beautiful daughter. Am I her Dad? Not at all. Now Jack has started to speculate about what it would be like if we had a child. FFS!

When we moved in together 10 years ago, we decided we wouldn't get a dog, since it would restrict our freedom. Now he wants a fucking baby? Sometimes he just pisses me off. Our friends Paul and Derek adopted a baby from Belarus a couple of years ago. He completely changed their lives - and not always for the better.

We both have demanding full time jobs, and it's hard enough for us to find time together. That's why we initiated Date Night - we stick by that religiously - we're guaranteed one night a month where we spend quality time together. Jack works in IT - no point asking me what he does, I've no idea. Of course, I'm a writer - you might have guessed.

We live in a 2 bedroom apartment in the Docklands - the second room is my 'writing space'. He usually leaves home at 7.00am for work. I'll sit and read the news online, maybe do the washing up. Come 9.00am, it's time for 'work'. I take a coffee in and switch on the laptop. It's the only room I'm allowed to smoke in. Some days it takes 10 minutes to start typing. Others, it might not happen at all.

Whatever he says, I know I'd be stuck looking after the baby, because he has to go out to work. I've no intention of becoming a Mammy, stuck at home looking after a kid, waiting outside the school gates, changing nappies. It's just not me. Potential crisis ahead!

Meeting Gloria

You'll be wanting to know a bit about Gloria. Jack and I would have date nights maybe once a month. We'd have dinner in one of the many cafes on South William Street. We really liked a small Italian place. I'm not going to name them because they refused to pay me for the publicity. Their loss.

Gloria always ate alone. She's an elegant woman. Well dressed, self-assured, great hair. Is that being sexist? I'm just admiring the woman. "What's the story, Rory?". Jack and I would speculate about her. One night we went in and the place was really busy. "Do you mind to share a table?" "No, that's fine" Well, he put us with Gloria, and we were so happy.

Obviously we apologised. We were brought up proper, Jack and I. It's rude not to talk to your table companion in that situation, so we did. Yes, she was 72. She'd been married to an Irish diplomat (sure aren't we all?), and had lived all over the world.

Irish restaurants, unlike European ones, don't encourage you to sit around when you're finished eating, and maybe buy another bottle of wine. Their loss again. Jack and I invited Gloria to share a bottle

with us nearby, and she was happy to join us. God, what an interesting woman. We were mesmerised by her stories of life on the Embassy circuit .
Jack and I would have date nights maybe once a month. We'd have dinner in one of the many cafes on South William Street. We really liked a small Italian place. I'm not going to name them because they refused to pay me for the publicity. Their loss.

Gloria Comes To Dinner

I've mentioned before that Jack is the cook in our relationship. No, we're not married, and never will be. We invited Gloria over for dinner one Saturday night. She looked as good as ever, and brought a nice bottle of wine. We were having one of those rare evenings when Dublin was basking in sunshine. We ate on the balcony (small as it is).

Gloria's husband George had worked in Irish embassies around the world. She had a wealth of stories to tell. They'd never had children - she felt it would be unfair to keep uprooting kids every couple of years. But they were really happy with their life. She was obviously devastated when George died a couple of years ago. She was determined, though, not to give up on life. Which is why she treated herself to her nights out at the little Italian restaurant. Jack and I just fell in love with her.

Gloria In Buenos Aires

I don't know how true Gloria's stores are. I just present them as she told them to Jack and I. Our monthly date night now always included her. We could just sit and listen for hours. The Irish Embassy in Buenos Aires obviously hosted a party for St. Patrick's Day. All of the Diplomatic Corps (Ambassadors or their representatives) would attend each country's National Day.

Gloria was in her element. She loved getting glammed up. Allegedly (I have to say that for fear of being sued), the Italian Ambassador, quite a dish she said, made advances. At this stage, she and George had been married for a while. Was she tempted at all? She said she was flattered, but not tempted.

Paris Was Made for Gloria

It really seemed the city was designed for Gloria - tres chic, tres elegant. She and her husband were there for 5 years in the 1970s, when Ireland when preparing to join the EEC. He was the trade attache so was heavily involved in those negotiations

Gloria never admitted to an affair, but Jack and I always thought she had one. She and her husband lived in a small apartment on the Boulevard St. Michel (kudos if you spot the song reference). She had lunch on the Champs Elysee with other Embassy wives. But she preferred just sitting in a small cafe on the Left Bank (I nearly said West Bank, which would be a very different story). She is a gregarious woman, and never short of company. She was fluent in French and Spanish, although her German was a bit dodgy. She credited the St. Louis nuns.

Gloria and George

Dublin in the 1960s wasn't exactly swinging. There was a low key but flourishing art scene - writers, painters, musicians. Gloria defied the wishes of the St. Louis nuns and opted to study languages at Trinity College. Her father was a well known surgeon, so money wasn't a problem. It was there that she met George. His father was a top official in the Dept. of External Affairs (now Foreign Affairs) and George hoped to get into the Diplomatic Service.

Of course, Gloria loved all the chic Trinity dance parties. There were the cafes where discussion of politics and art was almost compulsory. There were the lavish parties of the South County set. Her family lived in Sandycove at the time. They had a housekeeper and a part-time cleaning lady. It was from the housekeeper, Joyce, that Gloria learned to cook.

The counterculture in the USA might be decrying marriage, but in the Ireland of time, it was still very much the done thing. Gloria and George were married at St. Joseph's Church in Glasthule. The lavish reception was held, quite naturally, at the Shelbourne Hotel. They enjoyed a 3 week honeymoon in Tuscany.

George got the job he wanted in the Diplomatic Service (obviously Daddy had nothing at all to do with it). He wouldn't serve overseas, though, for at least two years. So they rented a small 2 bedroom house in Rathgar, and settled into their new lives.

Finally Overseas

George got his first overseas posting as a very junior staff member at the Embassy in Madrid, focused on trade. This was long before Ireland had joined the EEC. It was the era of General Franco, although foreign Embassy staff were largely immune from the military state under which ordinary Spaniards lived. Gloria, of course, was fluent in Spanish, and soon took a job at a school in the centre of Madrid.

It wasn't all glitzy Embassy parties. Neither of them were earning very much, and they lived in a one bedroom apartment not too far from the centre. Still, the lifestyle suited them both. Gloria finished work before George did, so had a couple of hours to explore her new 'home town'. She said it was here that she developed her love of cafe culture, just sitting and people watching.

They would meet when George finished work, visit the local market, and head home to cook dinner. A couple of times a month, she told us, they would treat themselves to dinner at a cheap neighbourhood restaurant. Un litro de vino tinto, some good food, listening to another world happening around them. They were very happy there.

After 2 years George was promoted and moved to the Embassy in Athens. They didn't have a word of Greek between them, so found this posting much more challenging. Again, they were living in a country ruled by the military. But they were young, resilient, and just wanted to explore a new culture. Gloria found a part-time job teaching English, and they were managing financially.

There is so much history and natural beauty to experience in Greece, and they tried to make the most of their time there. From Athens it was relatively easy to reach the islands or visit some historic site on a weekend off. As a cook, Gloria was in her element learning a new cuisine. They were able to host small dinner parties for equivalent ranking Embassy staff from other countries occasionally, and theirs was alway a popular invitation.

Soon though, they were approaching their 2 year rotation, and had no idea where they'd be posted next. Part of the excitement of being a diplomat's wife, Gloria told us.

'Home' Again?

George had 2 weeks leave before his next posting, so they decided to spend it in Dublin. We didn't know the Department of Foreign Affairs has a number of apartments in town for use by overseas staff for just these occasions. I suppose it makes sense. They were hoping to reconnect with some of their old friends from their college days. In the age before email, it was difficult to maintain friendships when abroad. Most of their friends were married and settled down, with kids at good schools, climbing those corporate ladders. Gloria admitted to being bored by them.

She said that was the moment they decided they couldn't live in Dublin full-time again. By this time, George had become something of an expert in international trade, so a move to Brussels seemed likely. He had a couple of meetings in the Department to discuss their plans. Ireland was trying to expand its exports, primarily in the agri-food sector, not just with Europe, but around the world. So it was off to Brussels.

It was another Department apartment (sorry!). Two bedroom, not far from the EEC headquarters. From watching news reports now, it would seem the EU was the only thing in Brussels. Gloria assured us it wasn't. Although one of Europe's smaller cities, it had a lot going on - a vibrant art and music scene, easy access by train to places like Amsterdam and Paris. Gloria chose not to work full-time, instead offering private English lessons to European bureaucrats and their children.

She told us they enjoyed their time in Brussels and were happy. There were quite a self-contained couple, although always ready to attend the next Embassy party. It was a good time for them.

A Price To Pay?

George was climbing the greasy EU pole. Financially, they were comfortable, but his job was demanding, and Gloria found herself spending more and more time alone. After a while, riding the rails to Europe's capitals, going to museums, eating alone - it all began to lose its attraction for her. She toyed with the idea of going back to full time teaching, but decided she was no longer motivated as in the old days.

She never said it in so many words, but Jack and I suspected she had a 'gentleman caller', maybe in Amsterdam. I suppose that would make her the 'lady caller'? How many times do you need to visit the Anne Frank House?

I suppose all relationships go through the hills and valleys. Jack and I haven't really hit a bad patch yet - something to look forward to, no doubt. This was Gloria's valley. A couple of years when she was unhappy. She kind of assumed George was having an affair, although she never knew for sure. Then, after 5 years in Brussels, he dropped a bombshell. He wanted to move on. What brought that on? Gloria had no idea, but she was probably ready to move on herself. At his level in the Department, he pretty much had his pick of locations. They spent a lot of time considering their options. Another big move was on the cards.

It's Pretoria Then

George chose to go to South Africa. Gloria was more than happy with this choice (they had actually discussed it - he didn't just arrive home one day - wife, we're moving to Pretoria). It was just after the end of Apartheid, Nelson Mandela was President, and there were huge export opportunities for Ireland to exploit. Gloria just loved being on a new continent.

They had an official villa, with a number of servants. It took a while for Gloria to get used to the idea she couldn't just go to the fridge to get a cold drink. That was a job for of one the house staff. After whatever had happened when they lived in Brussels, Gloria said she and George were closer than ever.

By now, George was a senior diplomat - with responsibility for Ireland's trade with Southern Africa - South Africa, Zimbabwe, Zambia, and more. There was lots of travel involved and Gloria loved exploring these new countries. She told us later that this was one of their happiest times together.

There were, of course, the Embassy parties, but also the safaris. She loved them, and was happy to take 5 days away to live in a tent. She made some good friends on these trips, and continues to be in contact with them.

Gloria In Pretoria

Mandela may have been President, apartheid no longer government policy, but racism was ingrained in South African life. Gloria, whose philosophy had alway been 'je suis un citoyen du monde', found it hard to deal with. She made an unlikely friend in the British Ambassador's wife, Joan. Their life experience was quite similar, moving around the world as a diplomat's wife. They tried to use their positions of privilege to make a small difference, ever mindful of the restrictions their husbands position required.

Gloria and Joan were both really interested in girls' education. They worked with a number of local groups trying to encourage girls to stay on at school, and to aim high in their ambitions. Gloria told us, though, that her favourite times with Joan were when they slipped away and spent a weekend together in Cape Town or Durban. A girlie weekend.

They were lying by the pool in a swanky hotel in Durban, eyeing up the waiters. It would be unthinkable for them to be seen out with these gorgeous men, but it costs nothing to look. Besides, they were both happily married. Michael was their favourite. He was from Zimbabwe, married with a couple of kids. He had a smile that just lit up his face. I think they both fell in love, just a little bit.

"Ah Shit", Said Gloria

The EEC was being transformed into the EU, and as the foreign trade expert in the Department, George was suddenly transferred back to Brussels. Gloria wasn't at all happy, but that's one of the drawbacks of foreign service. She was adamant, though, that they weren't going to live in the EU quarter of the city. She insisted on an apartment on the outskirts. "Fuck it", she told us, "if they're going to uproot me from my perfect life in South Africa, he can take a train for half an hour to work". Who'd argue with her?

While in South Africa, she'd become really interested in girls' education. She continued that by working with a couple of voluntary groups providing education to young refugee girls. She said that she found it really satisfying. She has a good heart. More importantly, she knew that education was the route out of poverty and forced marriages for these young women.

Of course, she was quite constrained in what she could say publicly. George was effectively the No. 2 in Ireland's negotiating team. You know when you hear on the news that negotiations between ministers went on until the early hours of the morning? Well, next time spare a thought for the civil servants who were up before the ministers, and when the meeting is over, have to try to make sense of what was agreed. George was rarely home. Again.

"And Then The Fucker Died"

They'd been back in Brussels for just 6 months. George was working flat out. Gloria got a call one afternoon to say he'd had a heart attack, and she should go to the hospital. They had an hour together before he slipped away peacefully. Devastated? Doesn't begin to cover it. Suddenly she was alone in the world, in what felt like a strange city. She was 62.

She was allowed to stay in the apartment for 3 months. Money wasn't an issue with George's generous pension. But where to go? Back to Pretoria where at least she had a friend in Joan? Back to Dublin where she hadn't lived for most of her life? In the spirit of trying something new, she chose Dublin.

She bought the apartment in Ranelagh, an area she used to know well. It seemed like an area that was actually developing - with lots of independent businesses such as cafes and the like. She tried meeting up with some old college friends but they bored her. She'd always been quite self-contained, and that stood her in good stead now.

As elsewhere, she enjoyed the museums and galleries, the theatre. Of course, she was really pleased at all the new restaurants popping up around the city. She would treat herself to dinner out maybe 3 times a week. Which is where we came in, and that's a white horse of a different colour.

Gloria's Home Life

Gloria lived quite close to us in Rathgar, in a modern 1 bedroom apartment. She invited us over for dinner one Saturday night. The apartment had lots of photographs and mementoes of her time overseas. We were to discover she was an accomplished cook - we'd assumed she couldn't cook as she usually ate out. She didn't like cooking for just herself, but loved entertaining guests.

Our €20 bottle of wine from Tesco seemed cheap compared to her wine rack. She cooked us a wonderful meal, with South American and Italian influences (remember that Italian Ambassador?). She was a hugely entertaining host. There was soft jazz playing in the background, we sat and ate, and maybe had too much wine. It was a wonderful evening.

Of course we had to invite her to ours a couple of weeks later. Jack was on a big beef kick at the time - only the best from Argentina. "But wouldn't it be better to buy local Irish beef?", I asked him. "Fewer airmiles". I was swiftly slapped down, since I obviously didn't know what I was talking about.

In my mind, he's a great cook. He's also good in bed, but doesn't vacuum or iron - you can't have it all.

Gloria arrived looking stunning as always, with an expensive bottle of wine from Chile. Yes, she'd been there a few times, and had stories to tell. She was impressed with Jack's beef (I beg your pardon?). The more time we spent with her, the more we loved her. She was worldly, witty and wise. Our dinner nights became an important part of our lives, and we loved them.

Meeting Mona

Since Jack and I split up it was harder to spend time with Gloria. She obviously wanted to stay friends with both of us. She and I arranged to meet for dinner in town one Wednesday night. I was surprised when she arrived with another woman. '"God", I thought, "she's not coming out to me?". No, this was her oldest friend, Mona. They'd been to the St. Louis nuns together, back in the black and white days. Somehow, despite all of Gloria's travels, they'd managed to stay in touch.

Do people still use the phrase 'a good time girl'? You could tell just looking at her that she loved life. "I've heard a lot about you, young man". "Oh really?" I said, a bit overwhelmed. "Oh really. Most of it was good, though. Now, we are all on champagne?" "I don't actually like champagne", I told her. "Oh dear boy".

She ordered a good bottle of Chianti for me, and champers for the ladies. It promised to be a lively night. "So you let that young man go? Gloria said he was quite a dish". "Well yes", I said, squirming a little bit. "He's very attractive. And a nice guy".

"You were together for a good while?". "Yes 10 years", I told her. "Ah, that's long enough for anyone. And if you don't mind me saying, you're no spring chicken".

Gloria intervened - "Mona is well known for speaking her mind". "I call it as I see it, and fuck the begrudgers. Which is probably why I've 2 marriages behind me". I had to laugh at that.

Mona and I

Were we being disloyal to Gloria? I didn't really think so. She was always invited. It was her choice to come along or not. She'd told us that Jack was going over for dinner on the following Saturday. So Mona called me and said that "we simply must meet". Who was I, a mere gay man, to refuse? I could see her as Diana Rigg in The Avengers, all leather boots and whatnot back in the 60s.

"I suppose you're too young to remember Bartley Dunne's", she said, when we were settled with our wine. No champagne tonight. "I've heard older friends talk about it, but no, I don't remember it".

"Well, it wasn't a gay bar, per se", she continued. "There were no gays then, just queers". "Oh right", says I. "It was theatrical dahling. All the Gaiety crowd drank there. Of course, the Abbey and the Gate were northside, so they wouldn't travel. As young women, out on the town, we loved it. No old men leering out over their pints of stout. Just fun and freedom".

"Not being rude", I said, "but what time are we talking about? Late 60s, early 70s?" "Indeed, the time of revolution in Europe. Mary Quant and Twiggy in London. A great time to be young. John Lennon and your woman sleeping in their bed on TV".

"It must have been an exciting time". "Oh it was. The stories I could tell you. But discretion being the better form of valour, or whatever that cliche is, I won't. At least, not until we've had another of these Rioja. It's quite good, don't you think? Reminds me of my 2nd husband. He was from Parma, where the ham comes from". I had a feeling we were in for a long night.

Jack Wants To Meet

I got a call from Gloria on the following Monday, asking to meet me for coffee. There was nothing very unusual about that. We met at a small coffee shop on George's Street. We are both strong black coffee drinkers. "You know Jack was over on Saturday night?". "Yes", I said, "how is he?". "To be honest, not good". "Oh", was all I could think to say. I decided this conversation would probably require wine. Gloria stuck with coffee.

"When was the last time you spoke to him?". "A couple of weeks ago, about the mortgage". "Well, he really wants to see you".

"I don't know if that's a good idea", I said, playing for time. "He really misses you". "And I miss him". "Oh, do you really?".

"Of course", I replied, "we were together a long time". "He's really struggling on his own". "Financially?" I asked, surprised.

"Oh don't be so dim. Struggling emotionally," she said. "I'm sorry to hear that, but I don't know how meeting him would help", I told her. "I think he wants us to get back together, and I don't. It's as simple as that".

"Look, you know I care about both of you". I nodded. "So please, see him just once. A couple of drinks. What harm can it do?" "I honestly don't know", I told her, "I'll have to think about it". For the next few days I thought of little else.

A Second Opinion

I decided to give Mona a call. "Oh, Gloria was always a romantic", she said. We were in a little tapas bar in town. "She thinks that, because she had such a good life with George, everyone else can too. Well, not in my experience, dear".

"So, you don't think I should see him?". "Of course, it's your decision. But what would be the point? For either of you?" She was echoing my own thoughts. "Unless you want to get together again?". "No, I'm sure about that".

"It's obvious you still care for him. And so you should. But you can't go back. Life isn't like that. You move forward", she told me. "You're right", I said, "I'll call him tomorrow".

I could hear the stupid dog barking in the background. "Hang on", said Jack, "Lola goes mad when the phone rings. I'll go out on the balcony". 'I remember it well', I thought, 'not one of her most endearing qualities'.

"Look", I said, cutting to the chase. "I had coffee with Gloria on Monday". "Ok". "She said you wanted to meet". "Well, yes, I was hoping we could". "And for what?".

"I miss you, and just wanted to talk". "Jack, there's no point. This might sound heartless, but I don't love you anymore. It's time for both of us to move on". There was silence. "Oh, I see".

"I know I've hurt you", I told him. "I don't want to hurt you any more". I thought maybe saying 'oh get over it' would be unnecessarily cruel. I waited for him to speak. It took a while.

"Alright, if that's how you feel". I could tell he was close to tears. I wasn't far off myself.

"I'm sorry, but it needs to end now. So I'm going to hang up". And I did.

A Surprise At Dinner

Gloria and Mona decided to take me to dinner for my birthday. I know, 42 - doesn't bear thinking about. We went to a lovely Italian restaurant in Ballsbridge which I'd never been to before. The girls were on champagne, naturally, while I chose a good bottle of

Chianti. I hadn't really been in the mood to celebrate, but they insisted.

We were just about ready to order when a surprise walked in. Yes, it was Jack. Oh, for fuck sake! I shot daggers at Gloria - she must have known. "Hi all", he said meekly. "Pull up a pew", Mona invited. Now he was sitting opposite me. God, this was going to be awkward.

"So you're the famous Jack I've been hearing about?", said Mona. She turned to me, "you said he was handsome, and you weren't wrong". Cue more squirming.

We finally ordered our food, but my appetite had disappeared. Mona was determined, though, to keep the mood light. "So Jack", she said, "are you younger or older than our birthday boy?" "A year younger", he replied. "I thought so".

The food arrived, and the table went quiet. Gloria and Mona tried to keep the conversation flowing, but they were fighting a losing battle. I'd eaten half my main course, and pushed the plate away. I stood up and said, "I'm going to call it a night. I'm not feeling great". Which had the benefit of being true. "Thanks for dinner, ladies and we'll talk soon". And off I flounced into the night.

The Wrath Of Mona

Mona called me the following morning. It didn't take a genius to know she was livid. "So, little man", she said, "are you over your hissyfit?"

"I'm sorry", I said, rather sheepishly, "I was just annoyed with Gloria for not telling me she'd asked Jack to join us". "And would you have come along if she had?". "Well, no". "Exactly". I hate when women do that.

“You owe her a big apology”, Mona said. “Me?” I thought she owed me one, but I didn’t say that. “Yes”, she continued, “Gloria went to a lot of trouble to get that table. Not to mention the expense”. “I know she did”. “So you need to say sorry. And mean it”.

“Look”, I said, “I’ll call her later, arrange to meet. I have a bit of work that’s already late, just a couple of hours worth”. “Well you just make sure you do”, she replied. “I’ll be talking to her later myself”. “Ok, I promise”.

“Brian, she’s really fond of you, as am I. But she’s also fond of Jack and has been trying to support him through this. She doesn’t deserve to be stuck in the middle”.

I finished the article I was working on, and called Gloria. We arranged to meet later that afternoon for coffee. Although in my case, I knew it would be at least a ‘one glass of wine’ job. On the way into town I felt like a kid again, facing my Mum or Dad after letting them down over something. It’s not a nice feeling at 42.

We were having a run of good weather, so I chose an outside table. There might be a lot of smoking involved. Gloria was on time as always, which is not easy when you’re relying on buses. “Hello Brian” she said. There wasn’t much warmth in her voice.

“Look”, I began, “I’m really sorry about last night. But Jack showing up like that just threw me off-balance”. “Indeed”. She wasn’t going to make this easy for me. “I know I hurt him badly”, I continued, “ which is why I thought it best for us not to see each other”.

“Well, at least we can agree on that. You did hurt him badly. But that’s between the two of you. I’m annoyed about how rude you were, to all of us, walking out like that. It was a very childish reaction. And quite frankly, I’m disappointed in you”. God, now I really felt like a naughty schoolboy. “You need to call him and apologise”.

Fuck it, I thought, I might as well go for the hat trick.

Queen of the (South) County Set

After they left the St. Louis nuns, Gloria and Mona shared the same South County lifestyle - the dances, the parties, the whole shebang. They were bridesmaids for each other. Each found a 'good catch'. In Mona's case, it was an up and coming solicitor, Peter.

They bought a lovely 4 bedroom house in Dalkey. "A bit more arty farty than Killiney", was how Mona described it to me. They were well regarded for their parties, at least until the 'set' started having babies. A French au pair was de rigueur. Mona insisted on a maximum of 2 children. Since Peter had no interest in kids, he was happy with that. They had 2 sons, 2 years apart, and each was signed up for a private school soon after their birth.

By now Mona was 30. She had the successful husband, the 2 'adorable' sons, the house in Dalkey, and the dinner parties. And she was bored. Going back to work was not an option. It would imply they were short of money (which they weren't). Peter worked in corporate law, and was confident of being called to the Bar within 5 years. Criminal law might have the glamour, he said, but corporate law was where the big bucks were.

Naturally, they were members of the golf club, although neither of them played. As well as the tennis and rugby clubs. It was a social thing. She and Peter were at the golf club for dinner one Saturday night (their date night, we'd call it now). Gareth and his wife Julia were the new kids on the block. He'd just joined the local dental practise as a junior partner. The senior, Michael, was due to retire in 3 years, so he was guaranteed to take over then. Julia looked after their 2 year old daughter.

Mona and Gareth bumped into each other in Blackrock on a wet Wednesday afternoon. It was his half day, and she was bored.

"Would you like to go for coffee?", he asked, "get out of the rain".
"I'd much prefer a glass of wine", was Mona's customary response.
And that was the start of it all.

I Just Called To Say...

When Gloria left, I went to the pub on Pearse Street - reconnecting with 'my people'. Somewhere along the line I'd forgotten I was working class. Yes, it still matters. My Dad did shifts in a factory, my Mam cleaned offices on Dawson St. when she'd fed us our tea. There was no pretense here. People either liked you or they didn't. If they didn't, they'd soon let you know. Those that did would do anything for you. As I sat with my first pint of Guinness (Jesus, I'd stopped drinking pints years ago), I realised I missed all this. The banter, the welcome, the barman knowing more about you than your own family. I felt I was coming home. Oh, stop snivelling.

After 3 pints I went home to call Jack. "Hi Jack, it's Brian", as if he wouldn't recognise my voice. "Oh hi" without much enthusiasm, and who could blame him? Stupid dog was as annoying as ever in the background. "Just a sec", he said. Out to the balcony, I could see it clearly.

"I want to meet you for a drink", I said, which was not in the prepared script. "I was rude last night and I want to apologise". "Oh", he replied, clearly surprised. "Well, I can't tonight, I've no-one to look after Lola". She's a dog, ffs, she doesn't need a babysitter. No, I didn't say that out loud. "Can you not ask Megan to look after her for an hour?". Megan lived one floor below us, eh, him, and I knew she would just stick the dog on the balcony with a bowl of water and forget about her. "I suppose", he said. "Can I call you back in 10 minutes? I'll go ask her now". "Sure".

It didn't seem to register with him that stupid dog was on her own for 12 hours a day while he was at work, but hey, I'm not getting into that right now. "That's fine", he said a few minutes later, "I've left her with Megan. Where do you want to meet?" "Why not Bertie's?" The pub was named after a certain former Taoiseach. "Fine. About half an hour?" he said. "See you there".

When we broke up I hadn't moved very far, so was in Bertie's soon after hanging up. There was no Guinness - it was all craft beers that no-one could pronounce. Jesus, where had my Dublin gone? Cue "The Rare Oul Times". The last of the 'office crowd' - all those Google and Facebook types - were just finishing up, so I grabbed a table outside. I was drinking a Czech beer - memories of a couple of good weekends in Prague before I met Jack.

I allowed myself 10 minutes of not thinking, or at least, trying not to think. Jack arrived right on time, typical IT nerd, and ordered a glass of Chardonnay. I almost laughed out loud.

Jack Apologises

"Thanks for coming down, Jack". "No problem", he said, a bit suspicious about what was going on. "I want to say sorry about last night. I was incredibly rude to all of you". "Have you spoken to Gloria?" he asked. "Yes, we met this afternoon". "She was very angry with you, so was Mona".

State the bleedin' obvious. "I've spoken to both of them, and I think we're all okay now". I was feeling slightly pissed, which is probably why I was here, so I decided to switch to wine. I know, I make great decisions sometimes.

"Look Brian", said Jack, "I should be apologising to you" What? Why? "I shouldn't have just arrived like that. I could see you were shocked, and not in a good way". Now I was conflicted - glad that he agreed that showing up unannounced wasn't a good idea; despairing because he was blaming himself for my bad behaviour. I realised I'd always noticed that about him, but it had never really clicked with me before.

"For Christ's sake, Jack", I said, a bit too loudly, "this isn't about you. It's about me". Now we were both sounding like petulant children. I'd always been the 'adult' in our relationship and I needed to slip into that role again. "Look, I fucked up last night. I'm sorry I ruined the night for everyone. That's it. Now we all need to move on".

He looked a little stunned. He took a sip of his Chardonnay and reached across for one of my Marlboro. "Can I say I accept your apology?" he asked. "Just say what you want, you don't need my permission, for God's sake". "Okay, thanks for your apology. But I still think I have some responsibility." Jesus, give me strength. Count to 10, I told myself, lighting another cigarette, even though I had one going in the ashtray.

"This could go on all night. We've both apologised. Let's draw a line under it". "Yes, let's", he said. "You know I've really missed you". I screamed.

Mona's First Affair

Mona and Peter were at the golf club on Saturday night as usual. There was a private function on, so tables in the dining room were in short supply. Who should they share with only Gareth and Julia. Mona had already made up her mind, Gareth just didn't know yet. It was a convivial evening. Julia maybe had a bit too much to drink, but she didn't get out very often. They didn't have an au pair, just a babysitter who would only stay until 1.00am.

Out of politeness (morya) they exchanged phone numbers. Mona and Gareth happened to bump into each other going to or coming back from the loo (yeah right!). "Wednesday, same place for wine", was all she said. He just nodded, and it was set.

Mona felt more alive than she had for a long time. She asked Simone, her current au pair, if she'd change her usual half day from

Wednesday to Thursday. "Pas problem, Madame. Bien sur". So much for using English all the time. Mona hated being called Madame, it made her feel like a brothel keeper, but Simone insisted on it. She was great with the boys so Mona couldn't afford to piss her off.

She didn't want to seem too overdone for the afternoon meeting, so was quite subtly dressed. Gareth, of course, was wearing his suit. Not quite as expensive as Peter's. "Let's cut to the chase, I want to have sex with you", she said with her customary frankness.

"I kind of guessed that", said Gareth. "I didn't think we were meeting just for a glass of wine" "Look", she replied, " we're both men of the world. Well not literally in my case obviously". She realised she was beginning to witter on, from sheer nerves. "Relax Mona", he said, "we're on the same page here".

Normally Mona wouldn't be caught dead on the northside, or the Darkside as it was referred to at the tennis club. They went to a small hotel near the Phoenix Park. It wasn't much to look at, but the room was clean, and it would only be a couple of hours. Having become used to Peter's quite perfunctory attempts, Gareth was a revelation. Their two hours together just confirmed to her what she wanted.

Jack Apologises. Again!

I didn't actually scream out loud, although I wanted to. It was slowly dawning on me that I'd become a parent to Jack's inner child. Stupid dog had just been the last straw. "You need to move on", I told him. "But I don't want to", he replied. He didn't actually stamp his foot, but I knew he wanted to.

"Wishing for a different outcome won't make it happen", I went on. "You need to accept we're not getting back together". "But why?". He was starting to whine now, and I felt the desire to slap him well up inside me. I wanted to say: because I said so. Remember how you were enraged when your Mam came out with that? "I thought you loved me".

"I did, but things change, people change". "I haven't". "Yes, I know. It's me, not you", always room for one more cliche. "I'm sorry if I did something wrong", he said. "But I don't know what it is".

"You see, that's what I mean". He just looked puzzled. "Why are you apologising if you don't know what you did?" "Well, I must have done something". "You didn't". Was that a lie? Possibly.

"I told you - I changed. And now we both have to get on with it". I was ready to shut this conversation down. I felt a sudden need to be in Tony's bar in Pearse St, having a rake of pints. "Jack, I'm sorry for the way things worked out. But we can't go back to the way things were. Maybe someday we can be friends again. I've said all I can, so I'm going to leave now. I'll see you around". I hoped it was a more dignified exit than the last one. I breathed a huge sigh of relief as I walked away.

Jack's Mum - Never Mam!

Deirdre hated her name - she thought it was too working class. She still lives in the old family home in Dartry (no, dear, not Milltown). Jack and I had only been dating for a couple of months when I was invited for Christmas lunch. This wasn't the formal dinner which would happen in the evening. It was more of an 'Open House' where neighbours, cousins or whoever would drop by for an hour, eat some smoked salmon, and head home. I'd never had sherry before. I succeeded in not throwing up.

Deirdre is like Gloria in so many ways. Now a widow, she is always immaculately presented. She hosts regular dinner parties - to which Jack and I are not invited. She loves her month long cruise around the Med with a couple of her friends. We keep expecting her to come home with a young Italian or Greek gigolo in tow.

Jack's sister, Grace (named after a certain Princess from Monaco) moved out of the family home as soon as she could. She now lives in Cape Town with a German banker, Leopold, and a couple of kids. She rarely visits Ireland.

So when this mythical baby arrives, we can rely on Granny Deirdre to babysit? To return to the vernacular of my youth - can we like fuck!

A Date Night With A Difference

After a couple of months I decided to knock this baby on the head (not literally Gloria). I told Jack I wanted a Date Night without Gloria. He was surprised. He can be a bit dim sometimes. I settled on a Wednesday night, and told him he had to be home by 7.00pm or else. I didn't want to go to one of our usual haunts around the Docklands. Luckily, it was a warm summer evening and we could eat at a table outside. Nobody listening in, no music in the background.

Once the wine had been served and our food orders taken, he asked: "So what's this about?" I sighed.

"You really don't know?" "No", he said. Yes, dim.

"Are you happy with our life together?", I asked him, taking a slug of wine.

"Of course", he replied, looking suitably shocked at the question.

"So why do you want to change it?". "I don't", he said, still struggling to understand what I was talking about.

"You want a child" "Oh, that's what this is about". Sound of penny dropping.

"Well, we're a great couple", he started off.

"Yes, we are. But you want to change our lives"

"I think we'd make great parents". "Do you indeed?", I asked. "And when were you going to mention this to me?"

"Well, we've both been really busy lately", he said, lamely. "Exactly, so who the fuck would look after this baby when we're both busy? Your mother? Ha!"

"But Paul and Derek manage". "When was the last time we had dinner out with them? Or even got an invitation to their place?"

"Yeah, I suppose it's been a while", he conceded. "Their son has changed their lives permanently. And in practical terms, it's all down to Derek. That's what would happen if we adopted"

Now it was his turn for a slug of wine. "And when were you going to ask me about this?", I said.

"Well, when we were having a good night out". "Which we haven't had for 2 weeks". He was squirming now, and God forgive me, I was enjoying it.

A Dog or a Child?

To be honest, I was just getting more angry. Normally we only argue about his failure to lift the toilet seat when he has a piss. Doesn't every boy learn that early in life? "So we can't look after a dog, but we can take care of a child? Are you deluded?"

"I was just thinking about it", he said. "No, you fucking talked to Derek about it".

"Oh, he told you". "No, he didn't. It was Paul. How do you think that makes me feel? These guys have been talking about it before I even knew it was on your mind?".

"I'm sorry", was his lame reply. "Look", I said, " we love each other, always have". "Of course".

"Well, this is make or break for us. I've never wanted a child, and I still don't. You have a choice to make. Which is more important - me or this mythical baby?".

"Oh", was his only reply. I could see he was near to crying, which made me want to cry.

"I couldn't bear to lose you". Good answer. "Then you need to forget this becoming a parent shit".

"I just thought we could offer a good home to a kid who needs it". "No we couldn't Jack" I said. "We're too busy to take care of a child". "I suppose you're right". "Come on, just look at Paul and Derek. They have no life apart from that child".

Have you ever seen a crest fall? He was crestfallen, and we were both just pushing our pasta around our plates. "Look", I said, "I know how you're feeling. How would you feel about getting that dog? I'm home all day, and might enjoy taking him for a walk".

Ah, his smile just lifted my heart. There's always a way to make your man happy. This is what love feels like.

When Gloria Met Deirdre

In the 10 years that Jack and I have been together, Deirdre's only been to our place a couple of times. We decided to invite her over to meet Gloria. Maybe trying to show her we had at least one classy friend. They weren't that far apart in age, but very different in life experience.

Of course, Jack was in charge of the cooking while I hosted drinks on the balcony. Deirdre wasn't terribly adventurous when it came to food, so it was lamb chops. I could see the 2 ladies size each other up over their Pinot Noir. Jack had asked Gloria to tone down her stories (I thought he had a bit of a cheek), but anything for a quiet life.

Ah well, Dublin is a small town, after all. It turned out Deirdre and Gloria knew a lot of the same people in the South County set, and of course Deirdre was impressed with Gloria's connections in the higher echelons of Foreign Affairs.

When we sat down to dinner, Deirdre was surprisingly quiet, so Gloria filled in the gaps in the gaps in the conversation. Without dominating, she kept the chat going. Years on the Embassy cocktail party circuit, I guess.

They took 2 separate taxis home. Jack and I sat on the balcony, breathing a sigh of relief. Of course the final verdict would be delivered by Deirdre the following day. Just for tonight though, we thought we'd pulled off a successful night.

A Dog's Life

Sometimes Jack can be like a 10 year old. This is either endearing or irritating, depending on my mood. "I'd love a puppy", he said a couple of nights later. This was going to be irritating. "No", I told him, putting my foot down. "You can't put a nappy on a pup, and I'm not cleaning up piss and shit all day".

"Oh right", he conceded. "Look, we'll head out to Dogs Trust and see what they have". "Great". Endearing again.

In case you think I'm a heartless bastard, I actually like dogs, and was looking forward to this. We went out to the centre just past Finglas the following Saturday. We had to go through an interview about our lifestyle - jeez, it's only a feckin' dog!. The fact that I'm at home all day was a big plus. I needed a dog, though, that was a bit self-sufficient.

We were introduced to a small Lurcher. I'd never heard of that breed before. They're smaller than a greyhound and bigger than a whippet. Same 'family' though The home visit was arranged for the following Wednesday. Well, Jack went wild on the Tuesday night, cleaning (which he never does), spotting and removing potential hazards. He was irritating again.
Jack took an afternoon off work. The bastard couldn't do that when I had to go to hospital recently for tests. We were happy to have Lola (Barry Manilow fans!) just roam around the apartment, sniffing everything. Apparently dog's pee smells like bleach. Who knew? And they'll keep going back to that spot. So when she pees, don't use bleach, but another type of cleaner.

I have to say Keith was a lovely guy. We just sat and chatted for half an hour - although I'm sure he was assessing us all the while. He'd go and report back, and we'd know in a couple of days if we could adopt Lola. Well, we got a call later that afternoon - Lola was ours if we wanted to go ahead. We could take her home the following week. Jack nearly creamed his jeans.

Jack's Day Off

He never takes a day off, even if he's sick. He couldn't take a half day off when I had to go to the hospital recently (no, Gloria, it's not a man's garden problem). However, he could take a full day when Lola was coming home. Pissed me right off.

He'd dog proofed the apartment as much as he could - which meant I was constantly searching for things that had been moved. We'd agreed that we'd give her free rein for 24 hours, to sniff things out, as dogs are wont to do. Then he'd be back at work and I could set those essential boundaries.

We set up a little bed for her in our bedroom, and another in my office. We'd been told that Lurchers are quite happy to lie around all day - just need a walk morning and evening. I went to work at 9.00am as usual the following day. I closed the door and she soon got bored, and settled down on her blanket. This is grand, I thought.

I was writing a piece for Cosmopolitan and hit a wall around 11.00, so decided we both needed a walk. We'd been told not to let her off the leash for a couple of weeks until we 'bonded'. (Jesus, Gloria, it was months before Jack and I 'bonded', and we speak the same language!). Luckily, she wasn't constantly pulling at the leash, just content to walk at my pace. We sat a couple of times while I had a smoke and thought of Cosmo.

I thought to meself - "Self", says I, "this might work out".

Stupid Fucking Dog

I was still working when Jack got home around 7pm. Lola went wild. Forgetting that I'd fed her, cleaned up after her and taken her for a walk. He knows that if my door is closed he shouldn't disturb me. I let her out, and told him to take her for a walk. "And get a take away", I said.

I don't know if he walked all the time or just sat by the canal, but he was out for about 45 minutes and came back with pizza. I don't approve of feeding dogs from the dinner table. Lola got more of the pepperoni than he did. It was another lovely evening, weatherwise, and we were on the balcony with a nice bottle of wine. "So, you took her for a walk?" "No, I put her in a cupboard for the day. She seemed quite content".

It took a minute for him to realise I was joking. I told you - dim. "Yes, I took her for a walk", I told him, "I also fed her, cleaned up her shit and had a long conversation about rabbits".

"Ah, she's lovely, though, isn't she?" Sometimes this 10 year old gets on my wick. "You'll have the pleasure at the weekend", I said. "Two whole days to bond and clean up shit. Let's see how you feel after that."

"But we're going to Paul and Derek for dinner on Saturday". Penny dropping. "That's right", I said. I can be a bastard when I want to be.

"So who's going to look after Lola?". You could almost hear the gears in his brain engage. "Who indeed?" said I.

"We'll just have to cancel". "Oh no", I said, "I'm not cancelling. This has been planned for a month. You know how hard it is for them to get someone to look after the baby."

"Maybe we could bring Lola and just put her in the back garden". Paul and Derek live in a small terraced house in Glasnevin, with a tiny garden. "Well, maybe you should call and ask them".

I said before that I never wanted to be a father, but sometimes I felt like one.

"No you can't bring a dog into the house", said Paul on the phone. "You know little Yuri is hypoallergenic".

A little digression about Yuri. He was called after Yuri Gagarin (Google if you must). On the night they told us the name, I managed not to throw up - just about. Yuri's name would connect him to his homeland. Oh please.

"Well, you'll just have to go on your own", said Jack. "I can't leave Lola alone on her first weekend with us". Yeah, she knows when it's fucking Saturday.

"Fine, I'll go alone". I wasn't happy.

Lola Gets On My Tits

"The dog can't sleep on our fucking bed". I was livid. "We bought her a perfectly good (top of the range) dog bed. That's where she sleeps". Jesus, now I have 2 of them giving me sad puppy eyes. "Look, Jack, we agreed on this".

"I suppose", said the annoying teenager concealed in this man's body. "Good, that's settled then".

I went alone to Paul and Derek's place on Saturday night. They'd found a woman who would sit with baby Yuri while we had dinner. Derek's the cook in their family and had decided on a tapas-style dinner. Great, lovely little morsels in their tiny back garden. Just my kind of eating. They were obviously disappointed that Jack didn't show up, but I made it clear that particular discussion was closed.

I've really missed our nights out as a foursome - going out for dinner, maybe having too much wine, but lots of fun and laughter. So this is what being a father looks like? Not for me, thanks.

What Happened To Sunday Lunch?

Apparently nobody goes for Sunday lunch anymore. Unless you're working class and eating roast beef in the Red Cow or Joel's. No, darling, down here in the Docklands we do brunch. Oh give me a break. Of course the stupid dog (no more Lola) had to come. I thought to myself - "Self, lots of red wine is required here, and fuck tomorrow".

Jack was already in bed when I got back from Paul and Derek's the night before. Stupid dog was on our bed but not for long. We'd barely spoken this morning. I was still annoyed and determined not to make this easy for him. I don't actually know what I wanted him to say or do, just some gesture. Unfortunately, I'd gone out with the petulant teenager.

"I think you're being very unfair to Lola", he started. What? Unfair to the dog? "Sorry?" I said.

"You're not very nice to her". "Sorry?", I said again. Take a slug of wine and deep breaths. "She can sense you don't like her". Ah, ffs.

"Excuse me", straddling my high horse. "I feed her, give her water, clean up her shit, take her for walks. And she senses I don't like her?"

"She can sense your anger right now". I didn't know who I wanted to slap first - him or the stupid dog. I realised I'd be more likely to be reported for slapping the dog. Is this the society we've become?

"Look", I said taking deep breaths, "you wanted the dog, not me". "No, I wanted a baby". Silent screams in my head. "I'm going for a cigarette. Just think about what you're saying". A time out was definitely in order.

A Glass At Gloria's

When I got back from my cigarette - actually it was two - I said: "I'm going over to Gloria's tonight." "Oh, are we going for dinner or just drinks?" Mr. Dim. I'd called her during the break.

"You weren't listening", I said. "I'm going, not we or us". "What?" Oh please not again. "I'm going to Gloria's this evening. Alone". "Oh, why?" I wanted to shout: to get away from you and that stupid dog. I didn't. "I just want to talk her", I said. Another "Oh" was inevitable. Sometimes I feel I could just have these conversations on my own. Did I mention I can be a nasty bastard on occasion?

"So what's this about, Brian?", Gloria asked as I lit a cigarette. We were on her balcony, catching the last of the sun, with a couple of glasses of wine. "It's the stupid dog", I said. "Oh really?" she replied, not believing a word. "Tell me more".

"You know Jack wanted a baby?" "Yes, and you made the right decision in saying no".

"So I agreed to the dog". "Not a good move", she said. "What do you mean?". "You didn't want a dog, did you?" "Well, no, not particularly". "And now the dog is coming between you". "Well, yes". I was beginning to sound like Jack at his most incoherent.

"God, you boys are so predictable". Who, me? Me and Jack? The whole planet full of men?

"You wouldn't have a baby together - and I believe you're right in that. So you offer him a dog". I was beginning to squirm.

"And when he becomes attached to the dog you resent it". "Well", I tried again. "Well, nothing", she said. "This is a one word answer. Do you still love him?" Shit wasn't the one word she wanted.

Were We Finished?

I took a long swig of wine and lit a cigarette. "Well, there's your answer," said Gloria.

"What? I didn't say anything". "Exactly". Fucking women. "This isn't about the dog, and you know it". Silence seemed the best option. "We've become good friends, yes?" she asked. "Of course". "Well, good friends tell you the things you don't want to hear. It's been obvious to me since I got to know you both that you've become Jack's parent, not his lover". Jesus, this was heavy shit. Another swig of wine seemed the only option.

"I don't want to leave him", I said. "That's not the same as loving him. You've become comfortable in your role".

"Do you think I should leave him?". "It's not my place to say". But you just fucking did. I needed to walk. I thanked her for the wine and the advice. She was right, it wasn't about the stupid dog.

A Pint Of Plain

I don't remember the last time I went for a drink on my own. Jesus, what does that say about my life? I didn't want a 'craft beer', just a regular pint of Guinness. I walked into Pearse Street - to a pub I knew from a previous life. No conversation required. Want a late drink? You keep paying, I'll keep pouring. It used to be my kind of place.

Jack kept texting me, so I turned off my phone. Again, when was the last time I did that? Ah, I suppose the decision had already been made in Gloria's. I just needed to think about it. Actually, no - I just needed to not think about it.

"Haven't seen you for a while", Tony the barman said. "No, I was just thinking it's been too long". "So I'm guessing man trouble", says he. "Kind of", said I. "Ah, you need to get down here more often. Where you were happy. What was your chap's name? Tom?" "Tony". Ah shit.

"That's right, same as meself. I thought youse were in it for the long haul". "So did I Tony", I said, "so did I".

Ah, Let's Call It A Day

I don't know why all my childhood memories have me at 7 or 11. I guess I was happy at 7. Brother No. 2 moved home from Bermingham with his wife and new baby (well she was about a year old). I was 11 or 12. They got a house in Ballyfermot and the 4 boys set in to do it up. I was just fetching and carrying (I know, Mona, story of my life). I was allowed to try painting a door. Then Brother No. 1 said: "Let's finish this, and call it a day". I said "I think we should call it a door". My first joke. (True story).

Tony said to me: "Brian, you know I don't often say this, but I think you've had enough, and need to go home". I fucking hate a caring barman after a few pints. But he was right - I couldn't put this off any longer.

As I struggled to get my key in the lock I could hear the stupid dog scuttle off our bed. "Jack, wake up". "What the fuck?" "Wake up, I want to talk to you". "What the fuck time is it?" "Late, or early", I told him helpfully. "Ah you're pissed. Just come to bed".

"No, I want to talk to you". "Ah for fuck sake. Put the kettle on, I want coffee".

Luckily we always have a bottle of wine in the house. I sat on the balcony while Jack made his coffee. "Look Brian", he said, "it's 3 o'clock and you're pissed. Can't this wait till the morning?"

"Well, we're up now". You can't fault my logic. "So go on", he said, reaching for one of my Marlboro Lights. He very rarely smokes. Maybe it was a sign? Ah stop Brian.

"I'm moving out". There, I'd said it. "What?" "I'm moving out", I said again. Consternation is the word to describe his face. "Sorry?". At least it wasn't 'what' again. No, I'm not going to say it a third time.

"Is this about the stupid dog?" At last we agreed on something. "We can send her back".

"Jesus, it's not about the dog". I decided to stop calling Lola stupid - I think the point had been made. "So it's me?", he scrunched up his face. Well yes, but I'm not going to say that (I'm not a total bastard). "It's us", I said. Meaningless.

"Fuck it, I'll get another glass". Good idea. "Did Gloria say this to you tonight?"

"It's nothing to do with Gloria, or the dog. It's about how I feel". "Oh, and you don't love me?". Jesus, what a question. I knew we were both about to cry, but it had to be said out loud. "I'm sorry, Jack, but not any more". So we both started crying. Ah God, why does life have to be this hard?

He was the first to stop crying. I just kept sniffling. "Well", he said, "i suppose there's a couple of practical issues to sort out". Fucking computer nerd.

Mona's Bored Again

Their Wednesday afternoon trysts (that's actually the word she used) soon became as regular as bowels on Bran Flakes. Mona being Mona, this wasn't enough. Although she enjoyed the sex, there was precious little else. Gareth was a conscientious family man with a young child. So there were no romantic dinner dates in out of the way restaurants. No overnight breaks to a nice country hotel. She just wanted more.

Happily, Gloria was back from Buenos Aires for a week. They decided to have a girlie break in Galway for a couple of days, to catch up on all the things that didn't make it into their letters. She assumed Gloria had already had her first affair - she was convinced George was queer, hence no kids. Gloria seemed happy with her life, and that was good enough for Mona.

It felt almost like being students again. Drinking pints in the middle of the day. Having long chats about boys (or men, now). They hadn't seen each other for a year, so neither was being totally open. They glammed up for their first night out. They didn't want to go to a top end place, they wanted somewhere they could let their hair down and just be themselves. The receptionist in the hotel recommended a small French place about 10 minutes walk, and it was perfect.

Of course, they had to have champagne and oysters. They both commented on the cute waiter's bum, or the waiter's cute bum. He wasn't French, but from Edinburgh. That struck just the right note of oddity they wanted. Once they'd ordered, Mona decided it was time to mention Gareth. Get him out of the way, in a way.

"Have you ever had an affair?", she asked. Gloria almost choked on her oyster. "Me?", she said, when she'd finished coughing. "Of course not". Well, that seemed fairly definite. "Why? Have you?"

Mona sighed deeply. "I suppose I am having one". "You suppose? You're not sure?"

"Well yes, then", said Mona, "I am". Gloria sniffed gossip, as only a woman can. "Oh do tell. Anyone I know?" "Probably not, they're new to the club". "Golf or tennis?" "Well, both."

"Oh, I do hope he's a 20 year old Spaniard or French student here on an exchange", said Gloria, maybe revealing a bit of a fantasy she had herself. "Not quite", Mona replied. "He's a dentist". "Ouch!"

"Yes indeed", said Mona, feeling the fizz had gone from her champers. Not so Gloria. "So how long has he been drilling you?" The most hilarious remark she'd ever heard. "Oh please, Gloria, don't laugh".

"It was a few months ago", Mona began. "Peter and I were at the golf club for our usual Saturday night out. There was a party on, so we were asked to share the table. Well, you know us, alway ready for a different conversation. He'd just joined old Mr. McGrogan as a junior partner, expected to take over when McGrogan retires in a couple of years." "Oh God, yes", said Gloria, "I hated going to McGrogan. A bit of a lech".

"Yes well", continued Mona, slightly miffed at being interrupted. "Gareth and his wife Julia had just moved into Dalkey with their young daughter. They seemed a nice enough couple and it wa a pleasant evening. No more than that". Not entirely true Mona, she thought. "Anyway, a couple of weeks later I bumped into Gareth in Blackrock one Wednesday afternoon".

"What was he doing in Blackrock in the middle of the day?" asked Gloria. "It's his half day from the practice. He asked me to go for coffee but I suggested a glass of wine. And that was that". She sat back and lit a cigarette, confident she'd told the whole story. Of course, Gloria was in no way satisfied.

"So you had a glass or two of wine with a man on a Wednesday afternoon in Blackrock", she said, "it hardly constitutes an affair". Perhaps remembering the Italian Ambassador in Buenos Aires. "Well obviously that was just the start". Mona was feeling a little tetchy at this point.

"Well, go on", said Gloria, "what happened?". "We went to a small hotel on the Dark Side". "Oh my God. Really?" "Yes, Gloria, really. We couldn't take a chance on being seen, even though it was a Wednesday afternoon". "But the Dark Side, Mona".

"The hotel was fine, and it was just for a couple of hours". Gloria was hesitant to ask the question, but she did. "And? Was it good?" "Fucking brilliant, girl".

Too Much Truth?

They were both feeling a little delicate the next morning. They were having difficulty keeping their coffee down. The smell of grilled bacon wasn't helping. It was decided a hairy dog was the only answer. The poor culchie barman had no idea how to make a Bloody Mary. Luckily for him, Mona and Gloria were experts, eager to share their knowledge.

No stick of celery, but this was in the days before your 5 a day was required. The first one settled everything down, and the barman was eager to show off his newly acquired skill, so they had another. Ah, normality.

After the third, they felt they could face the day outside. It was bright, but not too warm, but they were girls of the 60s, so always had their sunglasses. They walked, slowly it has to be said, and after 15 minutes they were close to Spanish Arch. They thought they might manage a light lunch - salmon with scrambled eggs perhaps. They found a small Italian - a restaurant, not a man. A bottle of Prosecco seemed like the right thing to do. Of course, they couldn't bear the idea of pasta, so settled on a small chicken salad. It filled the gap. They felt like they were back in their student days - a bit naughty and decadent.

"So, Mona", said Gloria, lighting a Gauloises - they were at the coffee and brandy stage by now - "are you going to keep seeing your dentist?". "Ah, I don't think so", Mona replied. "It's all so routine, not what I imagined an affair would be like". She lit her own cigarette. "I suppose I expected a bit of excitement, danger even. But it's become like going to your Granny's. Routine. Now don't get me wrong, the sex is still good. But it's just not enough."

This calls for more brandy. "You're really not very happy with your life, are you?" said Gloria, stating the bleedin' obvious as we'd say today. "Are you?", asked Mona. "Well, it's not perfect, but yes, I am happy. I have a good life with George. A great social life in Buenos Aires. It's all good".

"What about kids though?". "Honestly", said Gloria, "I wasn't cut out to be a mother. So it's not something I miss. No, I'm very content with my life".

"Oh", was all that Mona could say. "Look girl", said Gloria, "I'm going to give you some advice. Take it or leave it, it's up to you. Firstly, ditch the dentist. It's just sex, and it's not going anywhere. And you need to think seriously about moving on from Peter".

"What? Leave Peter and the boys? I couldn't. We love each other". "Well, I'm sure you do, in a fashion. But we all know he'd rather share his bed with a 20 year old Thai boy".

Mona was genuinely stunned and speechless. "You don't know what you're talking about". "Mona, come on, you can't be that blind". Well obviously she must be if it were true. "I think I want to leave now", she said, "I mean, go back to Dublin".

"That's fine Mona. We've plenty of time for the evening train. "Can all this be happening to me?" thought Mona. Apparently, yes.

Mona Does A Shirley

Of course, we're talking about the time before Willy Russell wrote 'Shirley Valentine', but you know where we're going. They went back to Dublin and Mona swiftly dumped Gareth. He'd been quite enjoying their 'cosy little arrangement', and couldn't understand why she ended it. She didn't have the heart to tell him that he bored her.

Peter was a white horse of a different colour. Surely he wasn't queer? After all this time together she'd have spotted some sign. Wouldn't she? She just didn't know anymore. She felt like following The Beatles to some ashram in India, but that wasn't an option. Instead, she booked a week at a small hotel on Crete. She just wanted to sit on a beach in the sun, drink cheap Ouzo and Retsina, and not think for a few days. Of course, it's impossible **not** to think about something when it's the only thing on your mind.

She was sitting on the beach and thought of Gloria. Was she really that happy? She remembered their time with the nuns. Mona was the big, bold one. It was she who had dreams of travelling the world, she hadn't gone any further than South County. Was that all there is? One more Ouzo might not answer the question, but what the hell.

As the plane descended into Dublin, she was full of butterflies. Could she actually go through with it? Gloria was off living her perfect life, so wasn't around for support. She was going to have to do this on her own. "Come on, Mona", she told herself, "remember what the nuns said about you. Let's prove them right".

Confronting Peter

Of course, she had to give Simone extra time off for holding the fort. It was the weekend before she got the chance to talk seriously to Peter. She booked a city centre restaurant, this wasn't a conversation for the golf club. Nico's on Dame Street had been recommended by friends but they'd never got around to trying it. Well, tonight was the night.

It was all plush reds and Chianti bottles with candles. We'd call it pastiche today, but then it was chic. She decided to wait until after they'd eaten. Why ruin a good meal? When the espresso and sambuca had been served, she took a deep breath. Actually, she just breathed, it felt like she'd been holding her breath all evening. "Peter, I have an important question to ask you", she began.

"Yes dear, what is it?", God, he sounded like her father. "Are you queer?". She probably should have waited until he'd finished his sambuca - he almost choked on a coffee bean. "What a question", he said. "Where did that come from?". "Just say yes or no".

"Well, yes", he conceded, somewhat sheepishly, "I suppose I must be". "And do you have a young Thai lover?". He roared with laughter. Not quite the reaction she was expecting. "Mona, darling," he said, "you're in fantasy land now. A young Thai lover? That is just too funny". "But is it true?" "No, it's not. I don't know who's been filling your head with this nonsense, but it's way off the mark".

"Really?", she asked, puzzled now. "Yes, really", he said. "I've been seeing a young man from Sandymount, that's about as Far East as I've been". "Oh", she said, feeling slightly deflated. At least Thailand was exotic. But Sandymount? It was just down the road.

"I suppose Gloria told you". "Well, she had her suspicions". "Dearest, Gloria's known for a long time". "Really? She's never said anything until we were in Galway". "Well, you'll have to ask her about that, but I told her before you and I were married. Asking for her advice. She made me promise that I'd be discreet and never embarrass you. And I hope I haven't. I never wanted you to find out. I never wanted to hurt you".

Strangely, perhaps, she wasn't hurt. She had her own secret after all. Peter decided a good cigar would go well with their brandies.

The ritual of selection, clipping, getting it smoking, would give them a few minutes to collect their thoughts.

“Peter, I’m leaving you”, she said, when she thought there was enough smoke. She hadn’t meant to be so blunt. Maybe she could blame the brandy? It didn’t matter, it had been said now. “Oh” was all he could say. “I suppose I knew it would happen if you found out. Damn Gloria”.

“It’s really nothing to do with Gloria”, she told him. “Oh, she raised the whole issue, but I’d already decided before that. In fact, I’m kind of glad you have your young man. Oh, please tell he’s younger, not some old fart?” He laughed. “Yes, Mona, he’s younger than I am, although not by much”.

“Good, I’m glad”, and she meant it. “So if it’s not about me being queer, what is it about?” “Order more brandy and I’ll tell you. Now, I need the bathroom”.

Mona’s ‘Free’

I asked her, “It must have been hard to leave the kids, though?”. She was slumming it with me in Tony’s pub. “To be perfectly frank”, she replied, “it wasn’t. The eldest, John, had just started boarding school, and Robert would be following him. Peter got a full-time housekeeper, so really not much had changed. In fact, I think he felt a bit more free as well”.

She’d fulfilled a long term ambition and moved to Paris. She took a small room in a shared apartment with 2 English women. They helped get her a job in the language school they both worked at. The pay wasn’t great but it was enough to live on, provided she was careful. She’d never really had to think about money before - first her father and then Peter had provided well for her.

She enjoyed teaching the small classes every day. It wasn't a full-time job, so she had plenty of time to explore the city. She soon learned her way around on the Metro or bus. As Gloria would in years to come, she revelled in the coffee shop scene. A cafe au lait and pain au chocolat gave her permission to sit for an hour, observing her fellow Parisians. She'd always been interested in fashion, and this was the epicentre.

She spent hours visiting markets and second hand shops, picking up small additions to her wardrobe to give her 'the look'. It was something she would continue throughout her life. She didn't have much of a social life to begin with. She would occasionally go out for dinner or just a bottle of wine with her flatmates, Jane and Rachel. She was equally happy in one of the neighbourhood bistros, alone.

Paris is the 'city of love', but that was the last thing on her mind. She was enjoying her freedom, and didn't need a man to make her complete. Which is exactly when one is bound to arrive.

Mona Meets Jerome

The French don't really do a 'lunch hour'. A good lunch can extend over a couple of hours, with a good wine an essential part. Mona finished teaching at 1.00pm and had just been paid. She decided to treat herself, and walked to a little bistro she'd found. It was very relaxed, a neighbourhood place and the food was excellent. She allowed herself une demi-carafe de vin rouge. She felt she'd earned it.

The place was busy, which was fine with Mona, she loved the buzz. It meant, though, that tables were in short supply. She managed to snag one at the end of the terrace. Great. She was just starting her salade nicoise when a young man approached the table and asked if she'd mind sharing. She'd rather not, but since the place was so busy she didn't feel she had a choice.

It was a very small 'table pour deux' so conversation seemed inevitable. "It's another beautiful day, isn't it?", he said when his beer arrived. "Paris in the spring - where can be better?", she replied. "Indeed".

"I think you are not on holiday?", he said. "No, I live here", Mona told him. "Oh. But you are not from Paris?" "No, Ireland". "Ah", as if that explained a lot.

She took a few moments to look at him. He was late 20s she guessed, well dressed (well, he was French), and dare she think it, quite good looking. Her main course of chicken in white wine sauce arrived. She'd never been much of a cook, but loved good food, and this was excellent.

"Have you been in Paris long?", he asked. "A few months", she told him. "I teach English". "Well, if you prefer we can speak in English? I do quite well". "Fine", she said. And so they did. His name was Jerome, he was a computer engineer and was single. He was from the Loire Valley, and had been living in Paris for five years. She asked if he was working today, and he told her he was just back from a business trip to Nice so had a day off.

The sun shone and 'lunch time' became mid-afternoon. They were on their 2nd carafe of red wine, and Mona was feeling very relaxed. He had a great sense of humour, even in his second language. It began to feel that this is what she'd been dreaming about all those years in South County. A handsome young man, a sunny day in Paris, a carafe of wine. She allowed herself to be carried away, just a little bit.

Mona et Jerome

"I would like to invite you for dinner", said Jerome. "Oh, not tonight. I need to sleep - too much wine". "No, not tonight", he smiled, "you are not the only one feeling the wine. Another time". "I'd like that", Mona replied. He took his business card from his wallet and slid it across the table. "Just call when you are free". "I will".

"Now, would you like me to find a taxi?" "That's okay, I only live a few minutes away. I'll walk", she said, hoping that she actually could. "Well, please allow me to walk with you". "That would be nice". A man to lean on was maybe just what she needed just then.

It was a couple of days later when she called him. They arranged to meet at the same little bistro. She didn't want to seem as if she was trying too hard, so chose a fairly understated outfit. He was waiting when she got there, a carafe of wine already on the table. Although the restaurant wasn't yet full, he had chosen the same table as at their first meeting. A touch of romance, perhaps?

He looked just as good as she remembered. They ordered their food, and settled in for the evening. Conversation flowed easily and roamed far and wide. He had a wicked sense of humour, which she'd always thought was important. By the time the brandy arrived, she was pleasantly relaxed.

"Mona", he said, "I must go back to Nice for a couple of days, a problem at the factory down there. I would like to see you again when I get back". "Yes, I'd like that too". She gave him her phone number and he promised to call at the end of the week. "Now, I'm afraid I have an early flight in the morning, so is it okay if I walk you home now?" "That's fine", she replied. "I have to teach tomorrow, so could do with a good night's sleep".

They walked slowly, as if trying to postpone the inevitable. When they reached her apartment block, he said "May I kiss you?" When was the last time a man had asked permission? It was soft and sensuous. She could get used to this.

Un Dîner Pour Deux

They were meeting at a small bar around the corner from Mona's apartment. She was a little early, and ordered a vodka and tonic. It was Saturday night and there was excitement on the Paris streets. Or maybe it was just in her head. Jerome arrived right on time. She admired punctuality - it was a sign of respect, she felt.

"I have been looking forward to this evening", he said, when his drink - Pernod - arrived. "Me too", said Mona. "I thought we could go to a nice, small restaurant I know, not so far from here?". "Sounds good to me", she told him. "Do you mind if I have one cigarette?", he asked. "Not if you give me one too". Gitanes, she thought, Pernod, yes he was French.

They finished their drinks and walked about 10 minutes to the restaurant. It was a lovely, cosy place on a quiet side street. The waiter was just lighting candles when they sat at a table on the small terrace as night fell. "May I order the wine?", he asked. "Oh, I think I can trust you". It wasn't a carafe of house wine, but a warm dark red from the Loire. Excellent.

The food was good, they laughed a lot, perhaps drank a bit too much. Mona realised she'd missed the company of a good man. And he was a good man - witty, entertaining, asking the right questions and actually listening to her answers. It was a really fun evening.

"Let's have one last cognac", she said when they reached her apartment. "If you're sure?". "I'm very sure".

Jerome woke her at 7.00am with a mug of strong, black coffee. "I am sorry to wake you so early, ma cherie, but I must leave now. I have a meeting at 9.00am". "Oh", said Mona, struggling to get her eyes open. "That's okay. You go ahead". "Thanks. I will call you tonight". "Yes, fine", she said. He pecked her gently on the cheek and was gone.

She sipped the hot coffee, and thought she might as well stay awake now. He'd left his cigarettes behind, so she she thought, why not? A fit of coughing answered that question. Being Sunday, it was her day off, and she usually went around the markets or second hand shops, but wasn't sure she had the energy today.

Deciding more coffee might help, she took it onto the tiny wrought iron balcony which was barely big enough for 2 chairs and a small table. The apartment was on the 4th floor, so the traffic sounds from the street were muted, except when that iconic sound of a police car could be heard.

She reflected on the night before. Jerome really had been charming and she'd felt more alive than she had for a long time, too long. He was a sensuous and gentle lover, and she wanted more.

Printed in Great Britain
by Amazon